For Eliza, Anna, and Kate

First U.S. edition 2010

Library of Congress Cataloging-in-Publication Data is available.

Library of Congress Catalog Card Number 2009014601

ISBN 978-0-7636-4680-6

2 4 6 8 10 9 7 5 3 1

Printed in China

This book was typeset in Rialto DF. The illustrations were done in pencil and acrylic.

Candlewick Press
99 Dover Street
Somerville, Massachusetts 02144

visit us at www.candlewick.com

Goldilocks
and the Three Bears

EMMA CHICHESTER CLARK

CANDLEWICK PRESS

Once upon a time, there was a family of bears:
Mommy Bear, Daddy Bear, and Baby Bear.
One morning, Mommy Bear said
"*Bother!* This porridge is much too hot!"

"Never mind, my dear,"
said Daddy Bear.
"Let's go for a stroll
while it cools."
But that day, as they
were leaving, a little girl
named Goldilocks came
by, and goodness, was
she hungry!

Goldilocks walked straight into the bears' kitchen. "*Mmm!* That porridge smells good," she said.

She didn't wonder.
She didn't ask.

She stuck a spoon into the biggest bowl and swallowed an enormous mouthful.
"*Eeuch!*" she cried.
"Disgusting and *cold!*"

Then she dipped a spoon
in the middle-size bowl.
"Whoaaar! Eeek! Boiling *hot!*"

Last of all she plunged
a spoon into the
littlest bowl.
"Mmm!" she sighed.
"Yummy!" she cried.
"This is *my* kind
of porridge!"
It was exactly right, so
she ate the whole thing.

After nosing through
the shelves, Goldilocks
found something to read.
"Now I need somewhere
to sit," she said.

She didn't wonder.
She didn't ask.

She plonked herself down
on the biggest chair.

"Yeeow!" she cried.
"What a horrible *hard* chair!"

She tried to get comfy in the middle-size chair.

"Oh! Too *soft*! Awful!" she groaned as she sank into the cushions.

At last she spotted the smallest chair. "Aaah," she sighed. "Bravo!" she cried. "That is *my* kind of chair!"

But . . .
snap!
crack!
It broke into pieces.
"Stupid thing!" said
Goldilocks, shaking
out her hair.

"I suppose," she said,
"there are beds upstairs."

She didn't wonder.
She didn't ask.

She climbed up onto
the biggest bed.
"Terrible!" cried
Goldilocks.
"It's much too hard!"

She leaped onto the middle-size bed. "Oh, save me!" she moaned. "It's so stiflingly smotheringly, suffocatingly, soft!"

"There's got to be something that's just right for me!" she grumbled.

And what did she see . . . ?

"Oooh!" she sighed.
"Bulls-eye!" she cried.
"Now that's *my*
kind of bed!"

It wasn't too hard
and it wasn't too soft.
It was as right as right
could be. Goldilocks
climbed in.

Meanwhile, the family of bears
had arrived back home.
"I'm hungry!"
said Daddy Bear.
"I'm starving!"
said Mommy Bear.
"And I'm absolutely ravenous!"
said Baby Bear. But . . .

"HEY!"
roared Daddy Bear.
"Someone's been eating
my porridge!"

"Oh, *my!*" gasped Mommy Bear.
"*Someone's* been
eating *my*
porridge!"

"Where's mine?"
squealed Baby Bear.

"Someone's been eating
my porridge, *and they've
eaten it all up!*" cried
Baby Bear.

"Oh, my poor darling!"
gasped Mommy Bear.

Then Daddy Bear noticed his chair.
It wasn't how he'd left it.

"*Someone's* been
sitting in *my* chair!"
he roared.

"Oh, my goodness!" gasped Mommy Bear.
"*Someone's* been sitting in *my* chair!"

"Mommy!" cried Baby Bear. "LOOK!"

"Someone's been sitting in my chair, and they've broken it all up!"

"That someone is a *hooligan* and a *thief*," growled Daddy Bear, "and if I find them, there's going to be trouble!" Daddy Bear marched up the stairs. Mommy Bear and Baby Bear tiptoed up behind him.

Upstairs, things were just as bad.

"*Someone's* been sleeping in *my* bed!" roared Daddy Bear.

"Someone's been sleeping in *my* bed!" gasped Mommy Bear.

Baby Bear ran to
his room.
"*Someone's been
sleeping in my bed,*"
cried Baby Bear,
"*and she's still in it!*"

"I don't believe it!"
growled Daddy Bear.
"It can't be true!"
gasped Mommy Bear.
But before anyone could
say another word,
Goldilocks leaped out of
bed. She was so frightened
her hair stood on end.

"*Help! Help! Save me!*" she
screamed, and ran away.

The three bears laughed and laughed and laughed. "I'll never know how a little girl like that could be so naughty!" said Mommy Bear.

Goldilocks ran all the way home, where she hid under her bed and didn't come out for a week. And she never poked her nose in other people's houses again.